Safe Keeping

Tara's Lesson in Responsibility

writtten by:
Tasha Gentles

ISBN: 978-1-4866-0866-9

Word Alive Press
131 Cordite Road, Winnipeg, MB R3W 1S1
www.wordalivepress.ca

Library and Archives Canada Cataloguing in Publication

Gentles, Tasha, 1979-, author
Safe keeping / Tasha Gentles.

Issued in print and electronic formats.
ISBN 978-1-4866-0866-9 (pbk.).--ISBN 978-1-4866-0867-6 (pdf).--
ISBN 978-1-4866-0868-3 (html).--ISBN 978-1-4866-0869-0 (epub)

I. Title.

PS8613.E558S24 2015 jC813'.6 C2015-900786-0
C2015-900787-9

This book is dedicated to my three beautiful girls who have made this all possible.

This Book Belongs to

____

It was a beautiful summer afternoon. The sky was clear, the sun was shining, and there was no sign of rainclouds anywhere. Tara was excited, for it was the perfect day to go to the big fair. She had waited for weeks, but between her parents' busy schedules and the bad weather, it never seemed to be the right time. Today her wait would come to an end, because the entire family was getting ready to go.

Tara and her big sister Timeira were upstairs when they heard their mommy call for them to come down. Both girls raced to their mother, anxious to know why they had been called.

As they made their way to the living room, where their little sister Tia was playing, they were out of breath.

"Be careful, girls," their mommy said as they almost ran into her. She placed a five dollar note in Timeira's hand. "This is for you."

Timeira's face beamed with excitement. "Thank you, thank you," she said repeatedly.

Mommy turned to Tara. "And this is for you." She placed a two dollar coin in her hand.

Before Tara could respond, Tia shouted, "Me too! Me too. Want money too."

"Oh, but you are too small to be getting your own spending money," their mommy replied.

Tara stared at the two dollar coin in the palm of her hand. She then glanced at the five dollar bill her sister was holding up to her face.

"Is this it?" Tara finally asked.

"Yes," said her mommy. "You both have your very own spending money. Remember what your dad and I have taught you about responsibility. Keep your money in a safe place, and if you see something really special at the fair, you can use your own money to buy it. Now girls, please don't lose it. Keep it safe so you will have it when you need it."

Their mommy then walked away, leaving the girls to themselves.

"I'm going to put my money in my wallet," Timeira said as she turned to climb the stairs.

"What for?" Tara asked. "That's no fun. Look what I can do with my shiny two dollar coin."

With all her strength, Tara threw the coin into the air and watched as it hit the ceiling and landed back on the floor. Tara laughed.

"I bet you can't do it with yours!"

She picked up the coin and threw it into the air again. This time the coin landed in front of her mommy, who had just re-entered the room.

"That's not being responsible," her mommy said to her. "I thought I told you to keep your money safe."

Tara stared at the coin on the floor.

"It's only two dollars," she replied. "I won't be able to buy anything with it."

"That's not the right attitude, young lady. You have to take care of the things you have, especially when you don't have to work for it."

Tara felt really bad that her mommy thought she wasn't being responsible.

"Sorry, Mommy."

She picked up her money, slumped her shoulders, and dragged her feet up the stairs to her room.

Tara looked at the money in her hand and still couldn't help but wonder what all the fuss was about. After all, this wasn't her first time getting money, and she'd never had to worry about keeping it safe before.

I don't think I want to be responsible, she confessed. *It's too much work.*

Feeling annoyed, she threw the money down on her bed. It rolled to the edge, fell onto the floor with a rat-a-tat-tat, and disappeared under the bed.

"Oh no!" Tara said. "Where did it go?"

She fell to her knees and searched for the coin on her bedroom floor.

"Tara!" her mommy called up to her, interrupting the search. "Please come down. We're ready to go."

"Coming, Mom. I'll be right there."

Oh coin, where did you go? Please come out so I can go. But there was no sign of the coin.

"It doesn't matter," she whispered to herself. "I won't be able to buy anything with it anyway. It's only two dollars."

So Tara gave up and made the decision not to tell anyone the money was lost, especially her mommy, because she might think it was deliberate. With that, she grabbed her bag and ran down the stairs.

They had one very important thing to do before they raced out the door. Daddy prayed that God would keep his family safe while they were away.

In the car, Tara's daddy explained that while they were at the fair he was responsible for keeping her and her sisters safe. He reminded them of the safety rules.

"It's important that we stay close together at all times," he said. "Never wander off or talk to strangers. If you get lost, find a police officer or someone who works in the park. But most importantly, don't wander around trying to find us. We'll find you. Understand?"

They all shouted a resounding yes!

At the fair, Tara was overwhelmed by all she saw. She'd been waiting for this day for a long time and now that she was there, she didn't know what to do with herself. There were so many people and so many wonderful attractions. There were dozens of rides and tons of different foods, an animal petting zoo, games to play, prizes to win, clowns performing, and face painting too.

"How will I decide what to do?" she asked.

"Don't worry," said her father. "We have all day to do as many things as you'd like. What ride would you like to go on first?"

"I want to go on the roller coaster. The big one over there." Tara pointed to the biggest roller coaster ride in the park.

Timeira wanted to go on the ride too, so she joined the line and waited for her turn.

ICKETS
TOWN

"I want to join the line too," Tara said hastily.

"First let's check and see if you meet the height requirement," her mommy said.

She measured Tara against the qualifying post. "I'm afraid you can't go on this ride."

"Why not?"

Just then, the really tall man operating the ride bent over. "I think you need to be a bit older to go on this ride," he said to her.

"But it looks like lots of fun," Tara protested.

"I know, but I'm responsible for making sure that everyone who rides this roller coaster is big enough to fit in the really big seats so they can be safe."

"Oh."

"Don't worry," replied the operator. "There are plenty of rides in the park for big girls like you."

YOU MUST BE THIS TALL TO RIDE
48
Hi I'm,

Tara was disappointed, but it wasn't long before she forgot about the big roller coaster. Her attention was drawn to the flying saucer. She then went on the Ferris wheel, the merry-go-round, the carousel, and many others. She went on rides with her family, and some she went on by herself. The bumper cars were especially amazing, because she was the driver and her dad was the passenger.

Tara had so much fun that she didn't remember anything about her lost money. She didn't even realize she was hungry.

"Can we go see the animals now?" she asked.

"We've been riding for a while," her mommy said. "I think it's time for us to have some lunch. Your sisters are very hungry."

"But I'm not! I would like to ride some more, please."

"Don't worry Tara," she said. "We will definitely go on more rides after we've all had something to eat."

When lunch was over, the family made their way back to the fair because there was still so much to do.

Suddenly, Tia started shouting, "I want that! I want that!"

Their mommy turned in the direction Tia was pointing,

"What do you want?"

"The cuddly panda bear!"

Tia gyrated back and forth on her daddy's shoulders in sheer excitement.

Tara looked and saw a really big, cuddly panda bear. "Me too, me too!" she said, joining in.

"I would really, really like to have one too."

Their mommy walked over to the young lady who was running the game.

"How much does it cost to win one of these panda bears?" she asked.

"Two dollars is all you need," she told her. "If you throw this ring around the bottle, the cuddly panda will be yours to keep."

"That's perfect!" Mommy said. "Tara, you can use your spending money to play the game. Since Tia doesn't have spending money, I'll pay for hers myself."

Tara had been having so much fun that she'd forgotten all about the money.

I can't let them know that I've lost it, she thought. In a panic, she said, "It's okay, Mommy. I'm a big girl. I don't need a panda. That's for little babies. Besides, we both don't need to have the same thing."

But Tara wasn't really okay, because she wasn't being honest. She had neglected to keep her money safe, and now she couldn't have a souvenir.

"Are you sure you don't want the panda bear?" her mommy asked.

"I'm sure, Mom," Tara said. "I don't need to have a silly panda bear."

Hi I'm,
Lisa

Cotto
STAFF

The family returned to the park and the rides, and it wasn't long before Tara forgot about the panda bear and the money she had lost. The family spent the day joining lines in the hot sun, going on rides, and battling with the crowds, so it was no surprise that they were all tired and finally decided it was time to go home.

Timeira then remembered she didn't have anything special to take home. She was a very good dancer, so when she saw a beautiful ballerina souvenir, she decided she wanted to have it.

"Mom, Dad, can I have that please?" Timeira asked, pointing to the ballerina.

Tara moved in closer to see what all the fuss was about. When she saw the beautiful ballerina turning inside a glass dome on tippy toes, she wanted one too.

"Me too! Me too! I'd like to have one of those," Tara shouted.

"Okay," Daddy said. "Let's go find out how much they cost."

The lady in the shop said that it was ten dollars for the really big ones, five dollars for the medium ones, and two dollars for the really small ones.

"That's perfect," their mommy said. "Timeira can have the medium one and Tara can have the smaller one, and you can both use your spending money."

Not again, Tara thought.

"It's okay, Mom," Tara spoke sombrely. "I don't want it anymore. Timeira can have it instead."

But Tara wasn't okay. She really wanted to have one for herself. She stood before the display table, staring at the ballerina inside the round glass dome. She saw how excited Timeira was with her new souvenir and how cuddly Tia was with her new panda bear. They both had something to take home, but Tara had nothing to call her own.

Tara's eyes welled up with tears until she couldn't hold them back any longer. Her mommy noticed that something was wrong and walked over to see what was the matter.

With tears running down her cheeks, Tara confessed, “I really want to have one of the ballerinas, but I’ve lost my money.”

“Why didn’t you tell me?” her mommy asked.

“I didn’t want you to think I wasn’t responsible,” Tara sobbed. “You told me to keep it safe, and I didn’t.”

“You don’t need to cry. Dry your tears. It will be all right.”

Tara cried even more.

“But I don’t have any money to buy what I want, because I didn’t act responsible.”

“A part of being responsible is recognizing what you did wrong, acknowledging that you’re wrong, and telling us about it. Then you should do all you can to make it right.”

$2
CAND

"I'm sorry, Mommy, for not being responsible and for not telling you that the money was lost."

"It's okay, Tara. Sometimes we have to get things wrong before we can get them right."

"What do you mean?" Tara asked.

Her mommy laughed.

"We make mistakes, but we get better the more we work on it. The most important thing you can do is learn from this mistake. Keep the lessons you have learnt safely in your heart so the next time you are faced with this problem you will know exactly what to do. The next time you are given something of value, you have to keep it safe."

"I thought I wouldn't be able to buy anything nice with two dollars," Tara said.

"It's not the amount that matters," her mommy said. "It's what you do with it, how well you care for it, and how wisely you spend it. We all have to be responsible at some point in our lives, and the older you are, the greater your responsibilities will be. Now, I'm going to make a deal with you. I'll use my money to buy the ballerina, and when you get home you can search for your two dollars. Then you can reimburse me."

"Is it okay if I don't make that deal?" Tara asked after she had thought about it for a minute.

"Sure it is," Mommy replied.

Tara saw the questioning look on her mommy's face, so she continued.

"I don't need the ballerina anymore. I would like to keep my money to buy something really, really special."

Her mommy was so proud of her, because she knew that Tara understood the lesson.

When they got home, Tara searched her room for her lost treasure—and you wouldn't believe what she found. Yes, it was the shiny two dollar coin. Her newly discovered treasure had been hidden behind her shoe under the bed.

She held it in her palm, and for the first time she appreciated what it was worth. She now understood that it wasn't the amount that mattered; it was being responsible and thankful for what God had given her so she could be trusted with more the next time.

She decided to put her treasure in a safe place, where it would never again get lost or stolen.

Remember, Jesus loves you!

www.ingramcontent.com/pod-product-compliance
Ingram Content Group UK Ltd.
Pitfield, Milton Keynes, MK11 3LW, UK
UKHW060115300726
14090UKWH00002B/203

9781486608669